Edward Abbott

The Baby's Things

A story in verse for Christmas eve

Edward Abbott

The Baby's Things
A story in verse for Christmas eve

Printed in Europe, USA, Canada, Australia, Japan

Cover: Foto ©Andreas Hilbeck / pixelio.de

More available books at **www.hansebooks.com**

" She lingered awhile in her favorite seat
By a window that overlooked the street." — PAGE 10.

THE BABY'S THINGS:

A STORY IN VERSE

FOR

...STMAS EVE.

...BOTT.

NEW YORK:

ANSON D. F. RANDOLPH & CO...

770 BROADWAY,

Cor. 9th Street.

I.

THE BABY'S THINGS:

A Story in Verse for Christmas Eve.

———•———

I.

THE December day was nearly done,
And far in the West the setting sun
Had tinged the clouds, as it passed them
　　　　through,
With many a grand and gorgeous hue:
This ere its fading beams should weave
The welcome shadows of Christmas Eve.

In a chamber that faced the glowing West,
A mother sat lonely, her hands at rest.

The work of the day had been laid aside,
And now, in the edge of the eventide,
She lingered awhile in her favorite seat
By a window that overlooked the street,
Silent and thoughtful, dreamy and sad;
Strangely so for a time so glad.
But the somber hue of the dress she wore,
And the look of sorrow her features bore,
Showed that it had been hers to know
The weight of a Father's chastening blow.

There she sat leaning and looking away
    Over the snow that covered the ground,
    Over the buildings that clustered round,
    Over the hills that rose beyond,
At the lingering sunset's rich display.

She watched the shapes as they came and went,
The sinking sun as his brightness spent,

And as she watched the scene seemed changed,
And forms and colors were re-arranged,
Until a glimpse, as she fancied, came
Of the heavenly city — Jerusalem;
The city that knew no setting sun,
No dawning day and no night begun,
The glory of God its unfading light,
And the Lamb that was slain its radiance
     bright.
Nor did fancy end its painting here:
The picture became more full and clear.
The cloudy masses that banked the sky
Were the walls of the city great and high;
In the glowing bars she would fain behold
The streets of the city of shining gold;
The fragments outlined with graceful curl
Stood for the several gates of pearl;
And the mellow twilight that round her shone
Seemed the light of the precious jasper stone.

Just one year ago this Christmas Eve
(How could the mother do else than grieve ?)
Her baby died—a beautiful boy ;
Her welcome care and her constant joy.
In an hour such as she little thought
The summons came, and the child was not.
The year had passed, but sorrow still
Remained the mother's cup to fill,
And now as the festal hour returned,
And her heart with fresh affection burned,
Her loss seemed greater than before—
Her burden increasing more and more.

So as she lingered and looked away
At the winter sunset's rich display,
The city which fancy had wrought afar
Out of cloudy bank and curl and bar,
Became the home of her angel child,
And the thought her sorrow in part beguiled.

A moment more and the sun went down
Behind the hills that engirt the town,
And its fading beams began to weave
The welcome shadows of Christmas Eve.

II.

II.

NEAR where the mother sat there stood
An antique bureau of carven wood.
Its corners were bound with plates of brass,
And its surface shone like a polished glass.
'T was a valued heirloom, one would say,
That had filled its place for many a day ;
Not strange was it then that she turned aside,
And the cherished relic tenderly eyed.

Ah! there was something dearer here
Than rich old wood and carvings queer,
For here the mother had laid away,
Out of the reach of every day,
Her baby's things such a precious store !
In her eyes sacred forevermore.

(19)

Oh, what a flood of reflections brings
The sight of a dear dead baby's things!
The snow-white slips, so simple and neat;
Socks that would do for a cherub's feet;
Blankets of flannel, so soft and warm,
Against the chill of the winter's storm;
Wrappers of muslin, so thin and cool,
For the days of the sultry summer's rule;
The jaunty cap, with its crisp rosette;
The quilted jacket of satinet;
The gossamer veil to shield the face;
The dainty shoes with their ties in place;
The zephyr sacks with their borders bright;
The cloak with its cape, so warm but
　　light;
Every possible color and hue,
Crimson and orange, purple and blue;
Oh, this was a wardrobe rich and fair
As ever a baby boy did wear!

" Thus sat the mother this Christmas Eve,
  Bending over the bureau drawer " — PAGE 21.

Thus sat the mother this Christmas Eve,
  Bending over the bureau drawer,
  Turning its contents o'er and o'er,
Examining every little sleeve,
Smoothing out fondly the flowing skirts,
Opening and folding the knitted shirts,
Sadly caressing the empty shoes,
Assorting the little socks by twos,
Spreading the wrappers upon her knees,
Stroking the blankets' silky frieze,
And dropping on every garment dear
The fresh perfume of a tender tear.
There they had lain from the very day
That the baby died ; and to give away
These things for some other child to wear,
Was a thought the mother could never bear.

True, they were useless lying there.
  She might never want them herself again.

Some at least she might easily spare,
   And let the rest in their place remain.
What a godsend even a few would be,
To many a child of poverty !

This had always been her thought before
   Whenever she looked the bureau through ;
   And to-night the thought returned anew,
As she handled the little garments o'er.
And seeing them placed in layers even—
   Without spot, or wrinkle, or any such
      thing,
   Smoothed as if by an angel's wing,
And cleansed as if by a breath from heav-
     en —
She was led to think of moth and rust,
Of thieves and fire and damp and dust,
And to feel that treasures are not enjoyed
Unless in generous ways employed.

There was Margaret Mills, the carver's
    wife,
Did ever one lead a harder life ?
Her husband's earnings were quite too
    scant
To supply in full their daily want ;
And with all her children now to rear,
Her time of sorrow again drew near.
What could a baby hope to find
   For itself in an already crowded nest ?
Its needs would be great, all hearts would be
    kind,
   But now there was scarcely enough for the
    rest.
Poor Margaret ! Many a heavy sigh
She had uttered, when no one else was
    nigh,
To think of the new life soon to come
Into her empty and cheerless home ;

And she wondered what she should ever
    do
If God should carry her safely through.

All this the mother remembered well
As she lingered under the bureau's spell.
In many a generous way, indeed,
She had proved herself a friend in need ;
And at this hour the thought would rise,
As she wiped the tears from her brimming
    eyes,
How much better every way 't would be
To follow the bidding of Charity,
And make up for Margaret Mills, poor soul !
Out of these garments a bountiful roll.
But no sooner did such a thought occur,
Than a motherly instinct would demur.,
She pitied the poor : she would gladly give
Of her ample substance to help them live ;

Money and time she would cheerfully spend,
And other assistance with pleasure lend
To relieve their wants and their sorrows ease
But she could not part with such things as
    these.

III.

" Over the sorrowing mother's soul,
Sleep and a vision gently stole." — PAGE 31.

III.

PONDERING thus the present and past
As the winter twilight faded fast,
Over the sorrowing mother's soul,
Sleep and a vision gently stole.
She seemed to have gone to a distant clime,
Back, far back, in a former time.
The hour was early in the night,
And the sky was filled with a wondrous light,
In the midst of which one shining star
Scattered its glorious beams afar,
While on her ear rose loud and long
A joyful chorus of heavenly song.
She had entered, borne by urgent feet,
A town on the hill-side. All the street

Was filled with a busy, roving throng,
Which hardly she made her way among.
Yonder she noticed a crowded inn—
Her ear could easily catch its din;
While just beyond was a rocky cave—
What a glory lit up its rough-hewn nave!
A mother was lying there at rest,
With a babe asleep on her pillowy breast.
Her husband stood wondering at her side,
Looking with love on his virgin bride;
It was—there was no mistaking *them*—
It was the manger of Bethlehem!
Yes, there were the shepherds out of the field,
Who had left their flocks with none to shield;
And there were the wise men out of the East,
Rejoiced that their pilgrimage had ceased;
The infant Jesus she really saw;
Was it strange that her soul should thrill with
      awe?

But strangely enough she seemed to see,
As she neared the sleeping child, that He
Who should call his own neither house nor
        lands
Was now without even swaddling bands.
   Her Lord in need?   In a moment more
   She had opened wide the bureau drawer,
   And (dreaming still) searched its contents
      o'er
With generous purpose and eager hands.
"There is nothing," she cried, "I would not
      spare
" For the Babe of Bethlehem to wear!"
And she dared to hope that the gift thus made,
And now at the feet of the young child laid,
Would be as worthy a gift from her [myrrh.
As the wise men's frankincense, gold and

A moment more and the vision went.

The mother woke with a sudden start.
The winter twilight was fully spent,
The moon had begun her slow ascent,
   And the heaven was starred in every part.
The scene before her had passed away
With the last dull tints of the parting day,
While instead before her very eyes
The figure of Margaret seemed to rise;
And at that moment she thought she heard,
Out of the stillness, the heavenly word:
" What shall it profit to say to the poor
" ' Depart in peace from my generous door,'
" While notwithstanding ye give them naught
" Of the needful things for which they've
      sought?
" If to one of the least of these is done,
  " Naked or hungry, a deed of love,
" It is done to Jesus on the throne,
  " And accepted by Him who reigns above."

Then the mother saw how her risen Lord
Stood ready to take her at her word.
If Margaret needed, it was *His* need ;
In *her* mute appeal she heard *Him* plead ;
Who could resist such a tender call,
When the sacrifice was so very small ?

IV.

" Down the snowy and blustering street,
Past the policeman on his beat."— PAGE 41.

IV.

Out from her dwelling, and down the street,
The mother hastened with eager feet.
She carried a bundle in her hand,
The happiest woman in all the land.
The plentiful snow lay all around,
And the wind rushed by with a dreary sound,
But she minded neither the night nor cold,
Her errand sufficing to make her bold.
Down the snowy and blustering street,
Past the policeman on his beat,
Under the gas-lamp's flickering light,
By the shop-windows frosty and bright,
Meeting many but noticing none—
Bent on her errand of love alone,

Over the river, icy and chill,
Along in the shadow of the mill,
And so at last to an alley-way,
Dark at best in the light of day,
Where, in a tenement old and poor,
Margaret lived on an upper floor.

Quickly she opened the outer door,
And ridding her feet of the clinging snow,
Made haste up the narrow stairs to go.
Up several flights and through the halls
She groped her way by the friendly walls.
Margaret's door she easily found,
And gave a knock with a ringing sound :
She was hardly surprised that the first reply
Which her summons met was a baby's cry !

Crowded the room—it must serve for all,
Father and mother and children small.

Kitchen and parlor, chamber and shop,
'T was long since the floor had known the
    mop ;
The plastering, cracked, had begun to drop,
The windows were narrow, the ceiling low,
  The air was close, and the only light
In the room was the fire's paling glow,
  Making itself by a contrast bright.
There, in the corner, Margaret lay,
With her babe beside her, born that day.
Poor little thing !   It had cried with cold
Before it was scarcely an hour old ;
Its lot had been cast in a dreary clime,
And its birthday set in a wintry time ;
And so what this mother came to bring,
Was like a breath of the genial spring.

Scarce a word was spoken. The babe she took,
And, pausing to give it one fond look,

Seated herself by the dying fire,
And deftly put on its new attire.
At work in his corner the father kept,
And the tired children all soundly slept,
Save one, who lying upon her bed,
So managed to raise her eager head
As to watch the movements, one by one,
Till the work of dressing was wholly done.
Then again the babe was laid to rest
Close to its mother's sheltering breast,
And when she beheld the garments fair
Which her little one was now to wear—
The knitted shirts for its body red,
   The socks for its twisting, curling feet,
   The snow-white slip, so simple and neat,
And the blanket around its furry head—
Her heart was filled with a sweet content,
And she said to herself: " The Lord hath sent
   His servant to me this gift to bear."

" Seated herself by the dying fire,
And deftly put on its new attire " — PAGE 44.

And her quick thanksgiving to heaven went,
  To Him who had made her wants His care.

But none the less was a pleasure given
  To her who had brought the welcome gift,
  And she felt constrained *her* heart to lift
In a silent, tearful prayer to heaven.
For it seemed to her that *to* the Lord
  She had made this gift this Christmas Eve;
Would He be true to His spoken word,
  She asked herself, and her gift receive?

V.

V.

THE hour was late and the town was still
    When the mother set forth on her home-
        ward way,
Out of the alley, and past the mill,
    And through the streets where the moon-
        beams lay.
But she minded neither the cold nor night:
Her step was firm and her heart was light;
For she thought of the babe of Bethlehem,
And held that her errand had been to Him;
Wondered that she had so long refrained;
Remembered her treasures that remained;
Discovered within a ready mind
Some other case of distress to find;

Saw how it was that they truly live,
Who, freely receiving, freely give;
And resolved that henceforth her life should
        be
To follow the bidding of Charity.

Dear reader, this world of ours is full
    Of just such mothers, and Margarets too.
To many, life is one long, hard pull,
    To others, a want would be something
    new.
Here is the over-stocked bureau drawer,
    And there is the empty, suffering home;'
Here of bread there is plentiful store,
    And there is the mouth beseeching some;
And to bring the supply to those who need,
The naked to clothe and the hungry feed,
Cool water to give from the springing well;
To go to the prisoner in his cell,

To visit the sick on the bed of pain,
The benighted stranger to entertain,
And wherever a want is seen to be,
To labor to meet it abundantly —
To do all this for the dear Lord's sake,
And the needed sacrifice gladly make,
This it is, surely, the Lord to please,
Even if done to the least of these.
Open then wide the friendly door,
Freely part with the treasured store,
Bend the ear when the suffering plead,
Give of the best to those in need,
Let nothing too good or too sacred be
For use in the service of Charity ;
And learn as one lesson for Christmas Eve,
" 'Tis more blessed to give than to receive."